CONTENTS

Heat Haze

Fay Weldon

A Phoenix Paperback

Not Even A Blood Relation first published in *Dempsters* in 1996

This edition published in 1996 by Phoenix
a division of Orion Books Ltd
Orion House, 5 Upper St Martin's Lane, London WC2H 9EA

ISBN 1 85799 752 2

Typeset by Deltatype Ltd, Ellesmere Port, Cheshire
Printed in Great Britain by Clays Ltd, St Ives plc

Stasi

I'd tell you the truth if I could, but I can't. No one can. 'Tell me what it's like,' you say. 'Tell me what it feels like.' How can I? No woman can speak the whole truth. She has her husband, her partner, her children, her parents to think of: there are always others to be protected.

Yesterday I read of a woman who finally met up with her son after fifty years searching. She'd been raped by a German soldier when she was sixteen. He'd fallen upon her in a Dutch cornfield, and left her for dead. But she came back to life and had a child to prove it. Her family turned her out; the authorities took the baby. You can never see him again, they said. Decades passed while she searched: the patterns of human cruelty and kindness changed; empires foundered and fell. Once she found someone who claimed to be her son but he turned out to be an imposter: the Stasi, the secret police, had stolen her boy's identity. She'd wondered why the adult's eyes were brown when the child's eyes had been blue. But all babies' eyes are blue when they are born, are they not? Deep, deep blue. In the end she found her true son; he was running a factory in Prague, in what was once Czechoslovakia but is now the Czech Homelands. Ah, home! Sweet and safe.

The fifty-year break was probably just as well. 'Mummy,

tell me what Daddy was like?' 'He was a fine upstanding man, darling, so strong and impetuous. See, I have the marks of his buttons on my ribcage to this day!' No, better to wait fifty years, for the scars to fade a little. A child must think well of his father, or grow up with a hanging head, a shuffling gait.

Can I give you some coffee? Yes, set up your tape-recorder on this table here. How nicely the sun shines through the windows. Yes, it is a pretty house: a little large and empty now for our needs: my mother says I'm throwing money away: is that my plan? – she thinks everyone must have a plan. Yes, I know the world is interested in how I feel. Yes, I owe the truth to my audience; yes, I know yours is a respectable and intelligent newspaper; but I must repeat there are individuals it is my duty as a woman to protect.

It is just as bad for men: I am not claiming special privileges for women. What father hasn't looked at his children and wished that he had chosen a different mother for them? Or wished them altogether out of existence, so he could be free? But he takes the same care the mother does not to let them know it.

Once we loved God, or our nation, or felt we would lay down our lives for this cause or that. But now that we have lost our capacity to love outside ourselves and must make do with the personal, we betray each other since that is all we have left to betray. I was betrayed by my husband, who kept a secret file against me in his head.

The secret police are everywhere; people prefer rules and penalties to be strict and unreasonable. Recently I was told the story of a French farming family at a time when they were living through the German occupation of their country. One day the teenage son turned up at Gestapo headquarters and reported, 'My father has a gun' – a capital offence. The sergeant, a father himself, said three times, 'Go home, boy. I don't want to hear this,' but the son persisted. Bureaucracy took its course. The authorities turned up, took the father away and shot him. So perish the disobedient, betrayed by the obedient: it's the asp in the bosom which gets you. The boy had his heart's desire, at least until he grew out of it. Which was, I daresay, the mother's undivided attention and no more disturbing noises in the night.

Oh yes, cruel and oppressive regimes have always benefited from the flow of children all too ready to tell tales against their parents. Ah yes, the informers are always with us: the neighbour who tells the tax-man all; the wife who shops the maid to immigration; the child who says his uncle fondled him. What ever changes? 'This person is really a Jew.' 'That person speaks against Stalin.' 'My nanny has Hutu blood.' There's always something. The interrogators get you, squeeze the truth out of you while you scream, inwardly or outwardly, be they the Inquisition with their rack and thumbscrew, the KGB with their truth-drug, the hospital saying 'and how did your child get that bruise?'

And then there's black-out! Black-out! 'I'm sorry, our records are private, our deliberations secret. This is for your own good.' Personal letters are censored in war, newspapers in peace: censors are always freely available: watchers are everywhere. Watch, watch, Neighbourhood Watch! Scratch away the apparatus of state, of tyrannical political systems, and we're left with our own natures: we have

3

social workers as our secret police; use teachers and doctors to inform on us; keep therapists as our bleak revolutionary ideologues. We cannot endure freedom. I read yesterday of a two-year-old, still groping for words, who got expelled from his nursery school, accused of racism. I tell you the Stasi is now in our own minds, no longer in the body politic; and the more frightening for that.

Do you take sugar? Milk? I talk a lot; yes, you're right – that way I need say very little. How astute you are. How old are you? Twenty-five, twenty-six? I love your wide belt; your thick, flowing, confident hair. Yes, I've seen your by-line. You are doing very well in the journalistic world. Married, I hear, and a baby, and a career? If you could choose any two, which two would it be? It might come to that. Quite often the choice narrows to one. But you don't want to know that. I shan't shove it down your throat.

No, I don't want my children to know the truth about their father. Truth itself is betrayal. It's everywhere. The mother protects her children: the children betray the mother, by leaving home and complaining about her for the rest of their lives. That is natural. Just as it's natural for boys to side with the father in any argument. Even if the father's beating the mother, and the boy stands there between them, taking the blows, the boy's feeling has to be 'Good, she deserves it. She's a woman. She should have kept him happy.' The lad can't help it; he just has to live with his shame.

Yes, let's get down to business. You're becoming impatient. You have to get back to give the baby its bottle. You have to keep the child-carer happy so she allows the baby to grow up to love you. Or whatever your guiding principle is. To be like you? Better than you? Happier than you? And you'll be going out to dinner tonight, and you can tell them you interviewed me, and what I was like. Keeping up a good front, I hope you will say. My hair is combed; I have my lipstick on.

Yes, my husband and I reckoned ourselves more fortunate than most. No, I don't think we were ever complacent. If you say so, yes, we were the world's most famous happily married couple. He wrote the films, I acted in them. No, I don't think there was a real conflict of interest there: I made more money than him but he had more status. I thought we balanced. Yes, I was wrong, as it turned out. Yes, our children follow in our footsteps: the boys acting, the girls writing. Yes, that reversal is strange. Yes, I like to say 'our'. That word is all I have left of my husband. But I'm probably a bit of a downer; not a bundle of laughs: he told me as much. Yes, I can see that after twenty-five years, so creative a man might want a change, to find some new source of inspiration. A touch of spirituality in his life. Yes, long-lasting marriages are unusual these days.

As you know, he had a threatened heart attack. As you may not know, being young as you are, the doctors and nurses gave him the new ritual advice, the viper-whisper they love to utter, the taking-aside, the word of permitting authority in the vulnerable ear, the Stasi sing-song which brings about the second, fatal heart attack sooner than anything. 'You must think about yourself now. Forget the others.'

That is to say, safer now to go it alone, since the source of the stress-related illness, the focus of all blame, lies in others, not in the self. But how does a man of integrity, a family man, a man who loves wife and children, if only by custom and practice, achieve such wickedness? To abandon all others and put himself first? The effort kills him.

Men are moral creatures, not just survivors. Some are prepared to die rather than say that black is white, that two and two make five. Dissenters have principle; torturers lack doubt. Everywhere the Stasi say that for the sake of others the disobedient must be tamed, must be brought into line, must abandon their random and dangerous fancies, whether they're to do with an anarchist cell, freedom of speech, or simply loving a family. The twist to the torture is the same in oligarchy or democracy: tell us what you know, admit that it was you, or we'll subject your children to this agony too. We know where you live. Do what we say, believe what we believe, or die. But in the doing, in the believing, in the saying, after the heart attack, lies the dying. They don't tell you that.

Yes, that's how it went. The story was in all the newspapers of the world, following where our films had gone. Why am I talking to you at all? I so seldom give interviews these days. I can't imagine how you got beneath my guard. Yes, the hospital sent my husband to a psychotherapist the better to be trained in the art of not loving me, the better to stay alive, the better to think only about himself. And yes, he made her pregnant, as everyone knows. Sex was part of the freeing process, as it now so often is. The cutting of the ties that bind. Yes, I can accept now that the pregnancy was accidental; neither one of them is alive to deny it or confirm it. What difference can it make? The fire that devoured the loins is quenched, if you don't object to a fancy turn of phrase. How long or importantly it burned for either of them is neither here nor there, though it seemed to matter at the time.

And yes, why do you ask, do you think I am foolish enough to reveal some little extra, some tiny scoop? Joanne Dee was found asphyxiated one morning, stifled with the pillow which had propped her patients' heads, she and her unborn baby dead. The big window which opened on to her garden was open. There had been a full moon that night. It must have been so beautiful, so bright, as Joanne sat and gazed at the trees silhouetted against the starry sky, and so forth and so on, and contemplated her achievements. What do I mean by her achievements? Why the severing of family ties, in which she specialised. 'A clean break!' she persuaded him. 'Make it a clean break.' The grass was damp with dew, but not enough to take the imprint of the killer's foot. And yes, I was arrested and charged with murder, and brought to court and acquitted, because where was the evidence? It could have been me, need not have been me. Any one amongst us could have done it; any of us who'd lost our family to her placid scheming, her smiling stupidity.

I sound as if I hated her? I do. Why? Because she rendered me powerless, because my anxiety and love for my husband made me helpless as she plunged around in our lives, destroying everything delicate and significant. Why can't I give up my hate? Because it sustains me. Yes, I hated her enough to kill her, but I didn't tell the court that. Of course I didn't. But I didn't kill her. I did tell them that. They believed me, why shouldn't you? Yes, I'm glad she is dead, and her baby too. He listened to her, not to me. She was the State, I the dissenter.

She was Stasi: she removed him for interrogation, went too far with her tortures, and killed him. Well, it happens. The second heart attack was fatal. Of course it was. The waxing moon saw his death; the full moon hers. My husband had turned up at Headquarters to inform against me, talk about me to a hostile stranger, as if I were not flesh of his flesh, bone of his bone, and he went too far. That is to say, he told her about our sex life, in detail, and so made nothing of it, before they'd even touched – though I daresay she thought about that from the beginning – and so the warmth of all our sex and love was not there to sustain him when he needed it. Bad-hearted, he fell, icy-cold, and stayed cold.

You ask me how I feel? I tell you the truth as best I can, a little portion of the truth, without upsetting new loves, existing children. On TV the other night I watched a group of former East German dissidents. They spoke of the stirring days before liberty was achieved, when free speech and free thought seemed more important than daily bread. One of their own, friend and comrade, confidant and lover, had revealed himself to be a Stasi informer. These innocents on TV, still stunned, shocked! 'How could he? How could he?'

'He believed in the proper authority,' said the man from the Stasi by way of explanation, 'and besides, we paid him well.' The woman the traitor had lived with went down to Headquarters, its files finally open, to see what her lover had said about her, to read his list of her feelings.

'What did you feel like,' asked the TV interviewer, 'to see yourself laid out and dissected in the Stasi files? By the man with whom you shared your life?'

'I felt as if my brain had been transplanted,' she said.

And that's what I feel like too. I feel as if my brain has been transplanted. Put that in your paper and print it. I am not the person I thought I was. All the years of my past are an irrelevance, nothing to do with me: there is no truth in them. I am negated. That can't upset the children too much, can it, to say that? I don't want them to start losing their jobs, their marriages, to hang their heads and start stumbling, like the political prisoners of long ago.

Not Even a Blood Relation

'**Y**ou are so selfish,' said Edwina to her mother. Edwina was thirty-one. She hated her name. Her parents had expected a boy: 'Edwin' had been ready and waiting. They'd just added on an 'a' and ignored her thereafter. Edwina was Hughie and Beverley's first-born. Hughie, Duke of Cowarth, father: Beverley, a fortune-hunter from New Zealand, mother. Now, decades into family disapproval, Beverley was sixty-one. Hughie had died three months back. Edwina had affairs, rode to hounds and drank too much. The family had just about got over the shock of the death. Now it was all wills, or rather no wills, and inheritance, or no inheritance, and who got what title: that is to say whatever sad crumbs of comfort spilled out after death could be picked over and scrabbled for. Hughie had been much and genuinely loved.

'But then,' Edwina remarked, 'you always were selfish, Mother.'

'What is so selfish?' asked Beverley, startled, 'about wanting to live in my own home?'

'Because it's far too big for you now,' said Thomasina. 'Sell the place and find somewhere small and sensible to live, and divide the money amongst us.' Thomasina was the second daughter. She'd been meant to be a Thomas. She was thirty. Now she was pregnant and had long blonde curls. That should show her mother a thing or two. 'Little middle tomboy,' her mother had once referred to Thomasina: cropped her hair short and tossed her a gun so she could join in the shoot. How Thomasina had cried. So many poor dead birds, falling about her ears!

'We must hear what mother is saying,' said Davida, the third daughter. Honestly, it was beyond a joke, and Hughie had never even laughed in the first place. He'd wanted a male heir. Davida was twenty-nine. She was a therapist, married to a psychiatrist. Her once bouncy hair had flattened out and grown limp from the strain of wisdom: her bright eyes had turned soulful: her voice gone soft from understanding her own anger, and that of others. 'In my experience it is counter-productive to cling to the past,' said Davida, 'though we must all find our answers within ourselves.'

Beverley's answer was to stay at Cowarth Court, on her own, all thirty-one bedrooms of it, three dining halls, two ballrooms, three bathrooms – hopeless, hopeless, one to every ten bedrooms, but the water supply in these Elizabethan mansions is always tricky, and at least Hughie and Beverley's *en suite* bathroom was properly serviced, plumbing-wise, and moreover warmed. In their childhood the girls had taken refuge with the horses whenever the weather got really cold. The heating never reached the nursery wing, but got to the stables okay.

Hughie had gambled and drugged the inheritance of generations away, spectacularly, with Beverley intermittently preaching prudence and commonsense. The girls had taken the father's side: Hughie knew how to live in style: Beverley, the feeling went, had the mentality of a New Zealand sheep-farmer's wife – which was what she had been born to, after all – all practicalities and no *panache*. Now of course there was nothing left to inherit. The family seat, Cowarth Castle, and most of its lands, had been hived off in lieu of tax into the National Trust's care ten years back. Only dilapidated Cowarth Court and a rather ugly Titian, both made over to Beverley by Deed of Gift during one of Hughie's bankruptcy panics, remained. But the moral right to these was surely the girls'. They were Cowarths, after all. Their mother was not really even a blood relation, not if you were talking Cowarth. Which they so often were.

But Beverley was proving remarkably stubborn. She declared she would live in Cowarth Court staring at the Titian – which was profoundly under-insured – just as long as she liked. She was unreasonable; the painting would bring in at least four million; they could all have done with their share – who could not?

'Royalty alone is allowed a female succession,' the family lawyer had once explained to Beverley, whose grasp of these matters was flimsy, no matter what her reputation as a fortune- and title-hunter. 'It's no use looking to them for example. Royal daughters are treated as sons so long as they have no brothers. George VI dies leaving two daughters: Elizabeth gets the throne and all the goodies. The younger, Margaret, gets zilch. Elizabeth's first-born is Charles; when Anne comes along; she'll only inherit if Charles dies without heirs. Then Andrew and Edward come along anyway to keep her in her place: she can forget it. But Hughie's just an Earl, so normal rules of primogeniture apply. That is to say, girls don't exist. Forget any thought of equal opportunity: male winner takes all. That's how such a mass of wealth gets totted up to these families over the centuries. Napoleon got rid of the system in France, zonks ago: great egalitarians, the French! Hughie being an Earl, you're technically a Countess, the girls are Ladies. If Hughie dies – heaven forfend, Lady Cowarth – without male issue the title and property, such of it as survives his life, will go to the nearest male relative: in this case Hughie's younger brother, John. Your husband is Lord Cowarth only because his elder brother died in a hunting accident – all too frequent an occurrence in this backwater of English society. First-borns tend to die; don't ask me to explain that.'

The original Charter from Queen Mary by which the Cowarths – Catholic stalwarts all – held their land and wealth laid down that what the monarch gave only the monarch (i.e. alas, the Inland Revenue) could take away. It had, in the form of the National Trust, done so. But under the terms of the Charter not even the Inland Revenue could have kept the inheritance away from a direct male succession. Torn between the risk of Hughie's bankruptcy and the risk of an intermediate heir turning up, the Inland Revenue chose the latter. The husband, after all, was Catholic, the wife well over child-bearing age.

'What option does an Earl without heirs have,' Hughie would boom, 'but eat, drink and be merry, and spend the lot! If you don't like it, Beverley, you should have given me a son!' (Three children in three years had finished off what little maternal instinct Beverley had in the first place.) In his apparently careless and scandalous contract with the National Trust, Hughie had ensured that if the girls got nothing, brother John would get nothing either, or only a title and he had one of those already. Hughie made no will, although he'd had six months' warning of death, leaving the tricky business of satisfying the girls entirely to Beverley. That too was his habit.

And Beverley came up with the idea of not attempting to satisfy the girls at all: simply keeping what was hers by legal right. The girls settled down to the situation presently. When Bevereley died, after all, Cowarth Court and the Titian could be sold, and the funds divided, and in the meantime their mother was quiet, and in mourning, and dwindling in a somehow satisfactory way; a thin, grieving figure in grand surroundings on a low income, wandering dusty halls, but at least maintaining the fabric: keeping the roofs mended and the chimneys cleaned. And the Titian was improving in value year by year. The girls would visit from time to time to see it was safe, and their mother well.

John failed in his inevitable legal battle with the National Trust. He didn't even get costs. Beverley was unsympathetic. 'You English nobs think you can live off your past,' she said. 'That's all finished, but you won't face it.' Which was a bit rich, the girls agreed, considering how well Beverley had done out of exactly that past. And not even a blood relation!

Exactly a year after their father's death Beverley asked her

three daughters to tea. She told them she had an announce-
ment to make.

'She's going to sell the house!' they rejoiced. 'She's going
to sell the Titian! She's going to move into sheltered
accommodation!'

The girls came together in Edwina's car, though fearfully.
Edwina was a ferocious driver. They were surprised to see
scaffolding up on Cowarth Court and workmen busy
everywhere.

'Where's she got the money from?' They were wild! 'Has
she made some deal with the National Trust? If she has, we
will have her declared incompetent by reason of insanity!'

But Beverley came down the steps towards them serene
and cheerful. She was out of widow's black and into a pale
yellow sweater and a very short skirt. She had on 15-denier
tights and the girls remembered how good her legs had
always been. Accompanying her was a short but good-
looking guy of, they guessed, around forty. Twenty years
younger than she. An architect, perhaps? A lawyer? What
was their mother up to?

'This is my fiancé Brian, said Beverley. 'We're getting
married next week.'

'Hi, Edwina, Thomasina and Davida,' said Brian. 'I've
heard such a lot about you lot. I guess your mother wanted a
boy!'

'You are completely disgusting!' said Edwina to her mother
later, on the phone. 'What will people say? You have
betrayed our father!'

'I know older people do have sex, but do you have to   15 flaunt it?' asked Thomasina. 'That short skirt!. And you were holding that man's hand! It doesn't bear thinking about.'

'Now Mother,' said Davida, 'you can't replace Father, so why do you try? You can only make a fool of yourself. Pop stars and actresses can get away with toyboys but a woman like you simply can't. You just don't have the style. Can't you be content to just be yourself?'

'They none of them know what kind of woman I am,' said Beverley to Brian later, in bed. 'They've only ever thought of me as Mother, something you draw the strength out of till there's nothing left.'

'Don't get upset,' said Brian, 'they were bound to take it hard.'

'If I'd been the one to die,' said Beverley, 'they'd have expected Hughie to marry again. And someone younger too. What's the matter with them?'

The girls wouldn't come to the wedding. No. They wouldn't.

'We don't have to get married,' said Brian, 'if it upsets everyone so much. Perhaps that's the answer. We love each other. I'll just move in and we'll live as man and wife.'

'Besides,' said Beverley, 'if I do marry you I become plain Mrs; Countess is out the window.'

So they didn't get married. The entire extended Cowarth family pretended Brian didn't exist. Beverley found herself marginalised. It made her angry. All those years of being on nothing but Cowarth sufferance! The male protection goes, and you're out, out, out.

'He's immensely rich,' said Edwina to her sisters. 'She's

done it again!' Edwina had set a private detective on to their mother's lover. He was found to be an Australian without education – he had made a fortune in computers, and now, no doubt – so typical of the *nouveaux riches* – felt he deserved to look at a Titian after a hard day's work. He had first met Beverley three years ago, one evening when he'd been installing – in his Ozzie hands-on way – the National Trust's great new state-of-the-art computer. Had their mother and this man been having a secret affair all this time? Was this why Hughie had got cancer and died? Suddenly, to believe anything about their mother, no matter how dreadful, became second nature to the girls.

'She used her title to trap him!' declared Thomasina. 'Why else should one of the world's most eligible millionaire bachelors' – for that was what Brian had been before she nobbled him – 'take up with a cowgirl from New Zealand?'

'She's a manipulative, greedy bitch,' said Davida, for once losing her cool. 'I hate her! She only didn't marry him so as not to lose her title.'

Oh, the girls were angry with their mother. But as children will, they soon settled down to the new situation. Brian gave them a few thousand pounds between them and they looked at him with more favour. At least their mother was too old to disgrace them by having a baby. She'd had a shot in the arm, that was all, of life, love and energy. Grudgingly, they thought, 'Good for her!' If Beverley left Cowarth Court away from them, or tried to give the Titian to her new lover or anything like that, they agreed they'd go to law.

'I don't know why they're all so difficult and moody,' said Beverley to Brian. 'It must come from Hughie's side of the family.'

Two years to the day after Hughie died, Beverley summoned her children again.

'I'm going to have a baby,' she said. 'There's a clinic in Rome does it for women of my age. They take away one of your eggs, fertilise it with your lover's sperm, re-implant it and Bob's your uncle. Or at any rate your little brother. Sometimes one has to use a surrogate womb, but they think in my case it won't be necessary.'

The girls would hardly speak to their mother. Sex at sixty was disgusting, but now to talk of a baby! Good God!

Edwina said she found something perverse about a baby emerging from withered loins: it was flying in the face of nature, the very idea made her feel sick.

Thomasina said poor little baby! It wasn't fair to it: its mother mistaken for its grandmother – even its great-grandmother – at the school gate: who would play football with the child at weekends? What happened when it found out its origins? The discovery could only cause unbearable trauma and suffering. She knew about babies! She'd had one. Society hadn't begun to think through the ethical implications of this kind of thing.

Davida said Beverley was being entirely selfish. She was trying to dance long after the music had stopped: it was pathetic; Beverley was sick in her head. For all her training, Davida said, she, Davida, just couldn't come to terms with this: it was too monstrous.

And the rest of the Cowarths said that to do such a thing was against God's will, or if God didn't exist – which as a family they increasingly believed – nature's plans for humankind. Hughie's widow, they complained, seemed indifferent to the fact that the Cowarths were, traditionally, a Catholic family. But what could you expect of a woman who used contraception and had thwarted Hughie of his heir and so driven him to his death? But Beverley was deaf to the lot of them.

She said to Brian:

1) It was no more perverse and unnatural to accept medical help to have a baby than it was perverse and unnatural to use penicillin to stop pneumonia. If it could be done what was the matter with it? Women commonly used HRT to postpone ageing: the menopause was not some sacred watershed, some divine punishment to women for their sexuality, just a gradual insufficiency of oestrogen. People just got hysterical about older women having babies. They became totally irrational and invented nonsensical arguments.

2) She was sure that if you asked the child at any stage in its life it would state it would rather be alive than not born at all. If it decided otherwise it could soon enough take itself out of this world. But it should certainly at least be offered the choice. Who was her second daughter, anyway, to seek to deny her fourth child life? Had Thomasina's childhood been perfect? No! Then by what right did Thomasina insist on perfection for others on pain of their death – or non-

19

existence, which was the same thing. Was it better to be met at the school gate by, say, an alcoholic, or an old mother? No-one stopped drunken mothers having babies: or ill mothers, or poor mothers; or only surreptitiously. And at least she, Beverley, could meet the child in a Rolls-Royce. As for the football argument, that was pathetic. What percentage of the nation's children were taken to football matches by their fathers, anyway? Precious few! What made Thomasina think they'd enjoy it if they were? Beverley was glad, however, that her daughter recognised the next baby would be a boy.

3) As for being sick in the head, she was not: she, Beverley, was profoundly sane. She'd given birth to three ungrateful and ungracious girls who had been mean to her from the beginning, despised her for her origins and taken their father's part against her, whenever they could. She wanted a fourth child. She wanted another chance. Fourth time lucky. Dear God, she too wanted a boy, and now medical birth technology made it possible, she'd have one. It might not be pleasant, it might not be easy, but she was strong, happy, wealthy and wise. And the nursery wing, thanks to Brian's money, was finally properly heated. If she tired or weakened a battery of nurses would be available to help, and though that too might offend some who felt only a mother's care would do, and a baby ought not to be born at all who couldn't experience it, her daughters had had her, Beverley's total care and were they grateful? No!

They chose to remember the things that went wrong, not the things that went right. The worm has turned, said Beverley, and I'm off to Rome in the morning.

It was as well that the Rome clinic had taken its fees in advance – hundreds of thousands of dollars – because on the way to Rome news broke of a discovery in the field of artificial intelligence that would eventually put Brian out of profit, and probably out of business altogether within the year.

Three years to the day after Hughie's death, Beverley stood on the steps of Cowarth Court, Brian by her side, and showed her new baby to her daughters. 'His name is Edwin,' she said.

They sulked, especially Edwina.

'But that's a Cowarth name,' they said, 'and you're not even a Cowarth.'

'This is a Cowarth,' said Beverley. 'This is Hughie's child and heir. Hughie had his young and healthy sperm deep-frozen years back, in case I died and he eventually remarried. It seemed the least I could do for your father, finally to bear his son – so this is the new Lord Cowarth.'

John's claim to the title was outdated. The National Trust lost its gamble and its claim to the Cowarth Estate. All now belonged to baby Edwin, and through him, in effect, to Beverley and Brian for the next twenty-one years.

'Just as well I didn't ever marry Brian,' said Beverley to her daughters, 'or the child would have been legally his, and not Hughie's at all, forget whose sperm was whose. Baby wouldn't even have had a title!' Put that in your pipe and smoke it, she could have added, but didn't.

Eventually Beverley married Brian and by reason of being mother to an earl continued to call herself by the courtesy title of Countess. The College of Heralds are still arguing the rights and wrongs of the matter.

In time the girls came to accept their little brother, and I'm sorry to say, respected their mother the more, if only for being so thoroughly selfish and bad. They certainly became far more polite to her, and agreed that it was their father's doing that their names were what they were, rather than their mother's, though without much evidence either way. As to their being obliged to shelter from the cold in the stables, had they not liked horses anyway? They were good girls at heart.

Heat Haze

I am coming to see you, Miss Jacobs, because my father fears I am anorexic. I know I am not. I am simply a dancer, so the less weight I carry the better, the less strain on muscles and joints. I am not self-destructive: I mean to live a long time and in good health. But I love my father very much, and if it relieves any anxiety he may have, I am happy to go through the motions of seeing a psychoanalyst, even in relation to eating problems I do not have.

Yes, I know you are not the analyst I will eventually see: that you act as a kind of clearing house for your co-professionals. It is your function to recommend me to someone you believe will be sympathetic: someone who will like me and whom I like. Though I am not convinced that in this field 'liking' is essential: some kind of intellectual rapport, yes. 'Liking' just somehow sounds kind of sloppy. But do what you see fit.

Yes, I am eighteen. Yes, people do say I am mature for my age, and composed. Dancing is discipline; and to discipline the body is, albeit inadvertently, to discipline the mind. And since my mother died when I was thirteen I have been very much in charge of my own life, and made my own decisions in most things, and on the whole have done it well.

No, I have no boyfriend in the sense you mean, though I

have suitors enough. Yes, I am satisfied with my appearance: ballet-dancerish; large-eyed, long-necked, long-backed, long-legged, a trifle boyish I suppose. If you stretch enough you don't get lumpy or over-muscled. A translucent look, true – but that comes from having a naturally pale skin; not I think from any nutritional deficiency. In this I resemble my mother. She died in a car accident, not from illness. I do not, you must understand, suffer from the self-doubt, the obsessional fears and the suicidal impulses which characterise the anorexic. But try telling that to my father.

Do I sleep well? It's strange you should ask me that. Actually, I don't. I need to, like a dog, but since last summer I've tended to wake suddenly, and very early, and not be able to get back to sleep at all. I hate it. It makes me feel I am not properly in charge of my own self-improvement. Lack of sleep is bad for concentration; what is bad for concentration is bad for dancing.

What happened last summer? Let me put it like this. I took a decision on my father's behalf, and carried it through in a way that quite shook me. I discovered a ruthlessness in myself which I fear I may inherit from my mother. What I did certainly smacked of the impetuous. Impetuously, my lovely mother ran across a road, and that was the end of her.

My family background? It was stable and ordinary enough to begin with. I lived with my mother for my first thirteen years. So far as I knew I had no father. We lived in a small house in a mean suburb; my mother worked as a secretary; all her earnings went on our subsistence and to see me through ballet school. She was not a typical stage mother, not the kind who vulgarly forces forward a talentless child, on the contrary. My talent had been obvious to everyone from the age of seven: my mother merely did her best for me. I suppose, in retrospect, that she had a tendency to the threadbare, to dramatic self-denial, to martyrdom. If we could make do with an old Brussels sprout rather than a fresh and more expensive green pea, we did. My dancing tights were darned, not instantly replaced, as were those of the other children in my class at the Royal Ballet School. Yes, the Royal Ballet School. I am as good as they come, I am told. If we could save money by walking, and not taking the bus, we did. Of course I was curious about my father, but he was absent to the point of non-existence. I assumed he'd walked out on us. I knew my mother didn't want him mentioned. I knew it would be risky. I always felt she and I were in a boat together, in dangerous and mysterious seas, and that if ever I rocked the boat, both of us were lost.

But when my mother died her sister was able to get in touch with my father readily enough. He turned up on the doorstep within days of the funeral. It turned out that my mother had quite coldly and ruthlessly kept my father away: she would let him have nothing to do with us. She had accumulated large sums in a dollar account; hundreds of thousands of pounds, which he had sent for my maintenance over the years, and which she had kept but refused to touch. These sums I inherited, but, incidentally, in time lent back to my father. Yes, his income fluctuates wildly; he is a threatre producer working out of San Francisco; his great love is The Dance, as he refers to it, though I wish he wouldn't. It sounds pretentious. But my father is very particular; he loves beauty, he loves perfection: for him The Dance exists as some kind of Platonic ideal. My father is no sort of dancer himself; that is the strange thing: my mother showed not the slightest aptitude. It is as if my father's absorbing interest has been inherited in physical form by me. It is enough to make one a Lysenkoist, a Lamarckian, and believe in the inheritance of acquired characteristics.

I don't think it is that I am miraculously well-informed, Miss Jacobs, I think it is rather that the rest of my generation is so badly informed. My mother and I had no television set; we borrowed books from the library. I daresay that helped.

Yes, of course I was upset by my mother's death. It was so sudden. Five years later, and I still dream about her. Whenever I buy new dancing tights I think of her, and feel guilty because I have no intention of taking up my needle and darning. I may be composed but I promise you I am not without proper feeling. Yes, I think I have properly grieved, and properly incorporated her into my being. I am grateful to her for giving me birth, and no, I do not resent her because she hid my father from me. She lived in one world, and he so very much lived in another. She wanted to protect me; she never could understand how little protection I needed.

The sudden appearance of my father on the doorstep? No shock or trauma there. Fortunately he is a very good-looking man so it was easy to accept him as a father. Good looks help in most situations, I find. He'd called from

Heathrow first, to explain himself. I'd thanked him for his interest, and for his trouble in coming all the way from the States: I asked him if he was married, if he was bringing anyone with him, and my father replied he was not married, since the law did not allow it, but he was bringing his lover. They went everywhere together. I tried to envisage her, but since I could not envisage him either, I failed, and perhaps just as well.

Two men turned up on my doorstep, hand in hand, not the man and woman I had expected. It was disconcerting for a moment, that was all. Many of the boys on my course are gay; or claim to be, or pass their adolescence as such. The acknowledgement of bisexuality, in my circles, is more and more common. I should not have been taken aback, but I was and it showed in my face. Bo said to my father, distressed –

'You should have warned her first: I begged you to but you wouldn't listen. You never listen!' and I could tell they were as good as married, and relaxed.

Bo was in his mid-twenties, African-American, gentle, kind, smooth-skinned, and a dancer too; I could tell that at once, simply from the way he stood; a body at rest, but with all the waiting energy of a coiled spring, and only at rest the better to prepare for that spring. I liked him at once; well, I am like my father; I adore beauty, and Bo is so beautiful. Besides, if he loved my father and my father loved him, that was enough for me. I could hardly claim exclusive rights to a father so recently acquired, could I? It might have been much worse, he might have turned up with some blonde bimbo on his arm, or a dowdy wife, he could have had six boring children; I'd still have accepted it. As it was I was elated. If I was perforce to do without a mother, obliged to have a new life, by all means let it be with a gay couple from San Francisco. My father was one of those guys with a bald head, a good moustache, and sad, humorous, intelligent eyes. Okay, so Bo was a young and beautiful show-biz boyfriend, so what. Well, yes, a few eyebrows were raised amongst the neighbours; they may have been an ordinary enough couple in California, but they came over as exotic up and down my very suburban street.

No, I repeat, I did not find the fact that my father was gay in any way traumatic. Many a man breeds a family before discovering his true sexuality. I am a rational person. For the most part what happens does not distress me: what I am does not depress me: I can see that Fate has dealt me many good cards. It's just that sometimes what I find myself doing disconcerts me, Miss Jacobs. And I wake too early. I need someone to evaluate what is right, and what is wrong. Or, in your terms, to differentiate between healthy behaviour and unhealthy, mature or immature. That's as pejorative, as judgemental, as you lot are ever likely to get. You're soft.

I decided to stay in London to continue with my training; I lived with my aunt – who fortunately had a less frugal temperament than my mother – and I was with my father and Bo during the summers. Either I went over to San Francisco, or they came to Europe, and we would tour the main cities, living in the best hotels. One meets little prejudice if one sticks to the centres, and can spend money. My father's credit was always good: it was only sometimes he had cash-flow problems, when I was happy enough to help out. It was his money, after all.

My Aunt Serena told me I had been conceived just before my father 'came out' as gay. When he told my mother she was sickened, angry and horrified; she was after all a child of her generation. She felt the best way to protect me was simply to wipe my father out of her and my life: better to pretend that I was an Immaculate Conception, than the daughter of what she saw as a pervert. My parents had met at a production of a Sondheim musical: it seems my father was trying very hard at the time to confirm his heterosexuality, but in the end failed. However translucent, however ethereal my mother, she was still too female for him. He did his best to honour his responsibilities in relation to both of us; it was my mother who wouldn't let him. Yes, he left her for Bo.

Why should I not be kind towards this cast of characters, Miss Jacobs? Why should I feel angry? Everyone did the best they could, according to their lights. Even the truck driver who ran down my mother was not to blame for what he did. She all but flung herself under his wheels. That's why I am so glad I am a dancer; dancing, like singing, is an activity that can't possibly do any harm to anyone else. And if I tire my body sufficiently I have no energy left to wonder why since everyone I know believes they are good, and does the absolute best they can considering the circumstances they're in, the world is in the mess it's in. Which otherwise might exercise my mind considerably. Seven hours a day at the barre, and you have little energy left for cosmic thoughts, thank God.

Last May my father called to say he was coming not with 29

Bo, but with Franklin. He had broken with Bo, after sixteen years. I was distressed, and told him so. My father said I would love Franklin as he did. Everyone must love Franklin. No, Bo had done nothing wrong: my father just felt it was time to move on. I felt cheated. Go to college and say 'my parents are divorcing' and everyone feels sorry for you: say 'my father's left his boyfriend' and you'll elicit no sympathy, only at best a prurient curiosity.

A couple of weeks later I had a phone call from Bo; he wept as he talked; I could not bear to think of his lovely eyes puffy and his perfect face swollen and disfigured. I would have preferred him to be composed, not to weep. His evident distress would do nothing to help him win back my father, who could not abide tears, or sulks, or disfigurement. To act blithe and make my father jealous would be much the better way, and I pointed this out to him. But Bo was too upset to listen to what I said. Franklin, Bo claimed, was a cheat and a liar; he would sleep with anyone or anything if it paid him to, he was very charming and very slippery: my father was completely taken in by him. Bo, in fact, spoke like any wife discarded in favour of a newer, younger model. I could not bear it; I wanted everything to go on as it always had since I'd met them: we three, through the hot summers, in perfect accord and harmony. I told Bo I would do my best to intercede with my father on his behalf, though frankly, I hardly knew how to set about it. I only knew I must.

Franklin took it into his head to call me from San Francisco the week before he and my father flew over. I did not like the sound of him at all. You can tell a lot from voices, and his was somehow greasy, as if truth could never get a proper hold of it. He said he did so hope we would get on, he thought he should introduce himself in advance: I was so important in my father's life; and now would be in his. He was so looking forward to his English holiday: he'd never been to Europe before; he hoped I'd found somewhere quaint and olde-worlde for us to stay; he'd heard our theatre was fabulous; he looked forward to fitting in a show or two. I saw no reason at all for the phone call, other than that he wanted to check up that I'd made the bookings. In the past Bo had simply trusted me, I booked as I saw fit, and I'd never let them down.

Intimidate other people? Who, me? I don't think so. In fact I think my trouble is rather at the other end of the spectrum. I am full of self-doubt. I lack assertiveness. I sometimes think I should go to classes. There are lots around.

I cancelled our hotel in Venice; I booked one deep in the English countryside. It was an olde-worlde hotel near Stratford-on-Avon, expensive, staid, and much favoured by Americans. I got us one double room, one single, and wangled seats for a couple of 'shows' through friends. Bo loved Shakespeare; so did my father: I was not so sure that Franklin would: in fact I doubted it. But shows he wanted, shows he'd get. I hoped his knees would twitch with boredom.

I met them at Heathrow, I drove them to the hotel. Franklin was attractive, I could understand why my father doted on him. He had soft, large, childlike blue eyes, and a very pink and fleshy, pouty lower lip; soft and weak. He was no older than I was. He made you think of sex. Bo made you think of matters more ethereal. Franklin had a high opinion of himself: he believed he was some kind of blond well-muscled Adonis; he looked to me like an up-market rent boy. Worst of all, was the soft voice which said whatever my father wanted him to say. And my father adored him. Franklin was a coward; we had to walk right round the car park to keep in the shade; he was convinced just a glimmer of sunlight would give him cancer. And he was very pale; the pallor you'd attribute to malnutrition, Miss Jacobs, but is just a particular skin type, like my mother's, like my own. The opposite end of the spectrum from Bo: perhaps that too was part of the attraction. For my father to have left my mother for black Bo was one thing; to leave Bo for white Franklin was another. This way, it seemed, corruption and self-deception lay. I felt what I had never felt before: that it was safer to be heterosexual; that homosexuality was inherently dangerous; that a love directed towards something familiar, not something apart, could the more easily be replaced by lust, and in turn be overtaken by the desire for sexual excess. You had to be careful, or you ended up in the bath house. And that there was indeed such a thing as perversion: conceived by narcissism out of the homoerotic, slithering out to pollute and infect everything around, and that my father was on some kind of slippery slope that fell away into – what? Hellfire? I had no idea, but I didn't like it, and I feared for my father, and someone had to rescue him. I had a sudden notion of the existence of Evil, in absolute terms. I had always thought of evil as an adjective, now I could see it was a noun, and a proper one at that, well deserving its capital letter.

The hotel was as stately and staid as I had anticipated. There was a willowed drive, and a Capability Brown garden, plus lake with swans. Franklin fell in love with it at once. The staff were courteous to the point of servility. My father and I put up with it; Franklin revelled in it. It was assumed that Franklin and I, who were of an age, were the couple: that my older father would have the single room. When it turned out otherwise, when the porter was asked to put the men's luggage into the double room, and my small suitcase into the single room, he did so, but hurried away. Pretty soon reception phoned through; Management told us with deep regret that it was against company policy for two men to share a room with a double bed. Management was embarrassed, Management was tactful, but Management was immovable.

Franklin was baffled. My father was aghast. I told them this kind of thing was not unusual outside London; I said the solution was simple. Franklin and I would share the double room: in the night my father and I would swap places. This we agreed to do. It was late, we were tired; the two men had flown a long way; simpler to give in than cry Homophobia! Barbarity! and walk out into the night.

It was hot. Indeed there was what amounted to a heat wave. Once prolonged good weather sets in over England it tends to stay, week after week. The sky was deceptively hazy, the palest of blues: nothing like the clear, bright densely blue Californian sky, of which I admit to not being overly fond. It seems too real, something actual, like a painted, arching ceiling, not the illusion, that accumulation of the next-to-nothingness of atmosphere, which 'the sky' actually is.

No, I had no particular feeling about leaving my bed so my father and his lover could share it. I am not hung up about sex. I just don't do it, if I can help it. I focus my sexual feelings into dance as a true priest embraces celibacy the better to realise the intensity of spiritual experience. This, to tell you the truth, is what worries my father about me: he being so much in denial of the possibility of a life not ruled by desire. And he thinks my loveless state must in some way be his fault. That by following his own passions through he has somehow prevented my own from flowering. Obscurely, too, he blames my mother for encouraging me to dance, in his eyes making matters worse. Parents seem to be like that. They blame themselves, or one another. I am prepared to take responsibility for myself. If I can't sleep, that's my doing, not theirs.

To continue. No sooner had my father laid his head on the pillow of his narrow bed in his quaint and olde-worlde single room, complete with false eaves and flower prints on the wall, than he fell asleep, exhausted.

'He isn't going to wake before morning,' I said to Franklin. 'I think we'd just better let him lie there, and ignore the bed-swapping routine. Besides, the air-conditioning in our room is better.'

Franklin agreed. We would share the double bed. It was only sensible. A soft night breeze blew in through the open latticed window, and played over my sleeping father's face, and refreshed it with all kinds of garden scents: I could detect lavender, and night jasmine, and violets. But Franklin slammed the window shut: and I suppose he was right: moths and mosquitoes came in a-plenty, as well as the perfumes of the night. Personally, I never get bitten by mosquitoes, a quality I inherit from my father, but poor Franklin suffered dreadfully; he was allergic to bites, it seemed. We left my father's room, in haste.

Now it had seemed to me from the occasional sidelong look that Franklin had directed my way during the afternoon that his homosexuality was a decidedly moveable feast. As Bo had indicated, he would do whatever he wanted with anyone, regardless of gender, if only he could get away with it. His soft hand lay frequently in my father's, but held in itself the potential to stray. I daresay this contributed to my father's obsession with him: that he loved Franklin a whole lot more than Franklin loved him. A middle-aged man, head over heels in love with a young boy. I didn't want to see my father as pathetic, I did not want my love for him spoiled by pity. It was obvious to me that my father existed in Franklin's life to further Franklin's interests: a leg up (and over) in the theatre world to bring him a fraction nearer to the stars, to yield up the cultural background Franklin knew he needed if he was to go far as a kept man, even in the city down the coast, in Hollywood.

Franklin lay naked in the bed; I lay naked next to him. It was too hot for covers. The window was closed, the air-conditioning hopeless. We both knew what would happen. Franklin of course had no idea of the degree of my calculation, my ill will towards him, my affection for Bo; certainly not the capacity for martyrdom I had inherited from my mother. To lose my virginity thus was the cold

Brussels sprout; to have kept it for a loving relationship the sweet and tender green pea I, like my mother, could not allow myself. And if I think about it my sleeplessness dates from this night. I have not really slept well since.

We lay thus for some ten minutes. Neither of us was quite prepared to make the first move. In these circumstances one does some instant bonding. And I must acknowledge that what I was about to do was not all that repulsive to me. Franklin did have a really good body. I could identify with my father sufficiently to admire it, to want to have it in sexual attendance on me. I do not want you to feel sorry for me, Miss Jacobs. Sacrifice it was, but to be a sacrificial victim need not be entirely without its pleasures.

I made the first move. I said, 'I suppose we ought to do what Management requires of us, in the interest of respectability and what people might think. We ought to fuck.'

At which, within half a second, he was all over me. He was accustomed: I know my anatomy: my hymen had broken when I was fifteen – I remember the occasion; I was at the barre: on points: my right leg stretching. Suddenly – well, there I was, married in essence to The Dance. But I'd known that anyway: certainly that I was betrothed. But now I considered the matter settled. Symbols come along to confirm a conclusion, not to initiate one. So Franklin had no way of telling I was a virgin: I will say that to you now, Miss Jacobs, in all fairness, though of course to my father at the time I had to cry rape: see what Franklin did, and me a virgin! But that was at breakfast, the following morning.

After sex, we slept. Or rather Franklin did. I opened the

window and let the mosquitoes in, and moved the sheet away from his body to give them proper access. I sat upright in the bed, knees to chest, and watched the thin, leggy things alight on the soft, clammy neck, the nose, under the eyes: with an eager wave of my hand directed them to the softest, most vulnerable places. The head of the penis, the armpit. The creatures alighted, settled, drove their poison in, and sucked, and lost their thinness and grew dark red, and Franklin slept, the pure sleep of the jet-lagged; and pink bubbles rose on his skin, even as the hellish blood-suckers I had summoned up departed, and the bubbles turned to red, tight, miniature volcanoes, and his manicured fingers moved to scratch the swollen tender places, in his sleep, and I was glad to see it happen. Franklin was, as he claimed, very sensitive, a mass of allergies. I rejoiced. I laughed in the light of the moon. Once they had served my purpose, I shoved as many flying creatures out of the window as I could; they flew heavily, engorged. I slapped a few others to death. Food slowed them up, more fool they. Then I closed the window, and lay down next to Franklin. I shut my eyes and dreamed of the possibility of love, and permanence, and the blessed ordinariness of an everyday life which could never be mine, but which had seemed to mark my father's life with Bo, and which I wanted back again, for them.

Why could it not be mine? Well, good heavens – I had given love up, Miss Jacobs, as a bad joke. I sacrificed my virginity on the altar of my father's welfare. Are you crying, or laughing? Crying? Good God! You're easily moved. I suppose in a way it is sad. I am like one of those walnuts, you know. Tough as anything: impermeably sealed; then 37 finally you break in, and what do you find? That the nut inside is shrivelled, inedible. All potential but destined never to grow. A walnut withered in its shell, that's me.

At breakfast Franklin was a disgusting sight. All crimson lumps and bumps on a white skin, disfigured, despairing, driven mad by his itching parts, one eye half closed, mouth so swollen he could hardly talk, let alone protest his innocence while I wept into my cornflakes and confessed what had happened between Franklin and myself. What Franklin had done to me. Seduced me, abused my innocence, taken advantage of my father's trust.

My father was sickened. When Bo called through to him later that morning, on my suggestion, the car was on its way to take us away, to the evident relief of Management. We were leaving for London: Franklin was being sent home forthwith to California, paid off; my father and I would summer in Venice. Where of course Bo joined us.

Why do you think I can't sleep, Miss Jacobs? Is it so wrong to interfere in another's life? To tell lies to a good end? To pretend love while practising betrayal? Was I not balancing Evil by creating Good? Isn't that what one's supposed to do? Was I not justifying my mother's disappointment, by keeping my father with Bo, making the trauma she endured worthwhile, if only in cosmic terms? When my mother ran from the house, so impetuously, it was because I had accused her of being ruthless and tried to press her to tell me about my father; and she was hurt. I hurt, she dies, he turns up. What's a mosquito bite or so on Franklin's white skin, a false accusation of rape, in comparison to that? So many questions! You can't be expected to answer them: don't try.

But that's why I am a dancer, and will stay so all my life. No longer a virgin, but that's about as far as my interest in sex will ever go. Work's a doddle compared to family life. I want no more of it.

Now that is settled, thank you and goodbye. Send the bill to my father. I will sleep well tonight.

A Great Antipodean Scandal

'How they quarrelled, Cordelia, Lord, how they rowed and raved! By night, the sound of their sobs and shrieks, slaps and counter-slaps, would rise through the clear Antipodean skies and make tremble the brilliance of the Southern Cross itself. That was back in the nineteen-thirties, when the heavens were pollution-free, and the constellations seemed infinitely far, and infinitely clear-cut. Nowadays the stars are nearer and muzzier. Those were the days when the Pacific broke its furious rollers against empty beaches, pipi-studded, and you could gallop a horse along the sands and not have to deflect its stride to avoid picnickers, or hippies, or a single jogger in a black tracksuit with a white stripe up the side of the leg; and there wasn't a café or a cream-tea in sight, or a 'This way to the bunjie-jump' or an old beer can either.

'New Zealand rose from the seas long ago after the rest of the world was formed: everyone, according to Harriette, was there by accident, even the Maoris, and the ocean seemed to know it. In the last fifty years the tides have become reconciled to the fact of New Zealand's existence, and break upon its shores more languidly. Yes, nature these days has lost quite a lot of its oomph: the spirit has gone out of it. It may be no more than the way a shiny haze of oil now coats the sea, the land, the sky, and dampens everything down. All that stuff that swilled about beneath the surface of the earth, unnaturally brought to the surface, like the damp of exhalation inside a balloon which is suddenly turned inside out.

'But that's just a fancy, isn't it, Cordelia? Whatever happens to nature, the babies still get born lively enough, burst into the world shrieking and furious. Yes, it's all you can do to get today's babies to sleep. I don't think the murmur of my voice will excite little Helen more than she is excited already. We could just go away and leave her to cry. No? You are storing up trouble for yourself later on, but never mind, that's only my opinion. I never had children myself. What do I know?

'What was I saying? Yes, how Reg and Harriette rowed! Your great-grandfather and -grandmother. They were famous for it, and forgiven, which was strange enough when you think of the community they lived in: in the little town of Christchurch, on the edge of the Canterbury plain, back in the thirties; the squarest place you can imagine, its very streets squared off as those of planned new cities are, fanning out from a town square with a Victorian church and a copper steeple turned green with age. Not very much age, in those days. Fifty years at most, but still the oldest building in the town, indeed in the whole country, except the Quaker Meeting House, which dated from 1840. Parties of school children would be taken to marvel at the antiquity of the Meeting House.'

'Antiquity', said Harriette to her daughter Pippy, in 1932, 41 'means the Greeks or Romans. It does not relate to some Victorian chapel in this dull colonial town. Remember that, Pippy.'

And she showed her daughter some white naked male Greeks dancing round a pale blue Wedgwood vase, a treasure she'd brought with her from 'home', England.

Harriette did not like New Zealand. That was mostly what she quarrelled with Reg about, though anything would probably have done as well. Reg loved the place. Harriette didn't. Pippy did. But then Pippy knew nothing better, as Harriette remarked: how can you miss what you don't know? Little Pippy, Harriette would complain bitterly to Reg, had even begun to speak through her nose, like any ordinary New Zealand child, afraid no doubt of opening her mouth properly in case a tuft of wool blew in. Canterbury lamb was the nation's export. First they were sheared, the poor pitiful plentiful things, then they were eaten. One sheep per bleak acre of tough tussocky grass. At shearing time, or so Harriette swore, wool blew with the hot south-western wind, blurred the eyesight, stuffed the mouth. Open it, and bleats came out.

By day, Reg and Harriette were as peaceable with one another as lambs: loving as doves – a species unknown in New Zealand, so the comparison was not often made. Only by night did they row, did they rant and rave, so that the sound of their quarrels rose to the Southern Cross.

'Noise never stops,' Reg told Pippy, who'd lie in bed on the verandah, listening to shriek and sob. 'Noise just leaves you and travels out to space; it goes on forever into infinity. Where there are ears to hear, it will be heard.'

'That simply is not scientifically true, Reg,' said Harriette, who was a doctor, but she never told Pippy what happened to noise.

A child can ask and ask, but if the question is simple it will never get a proper answer. In the end the child stops asking, feeling foolish, but the truth is that nobody knows. Where does space end? Why are we here? Where was I before I was born? Such a complexity of civilisation is built on ignorance.

'Reg edited the Christchurch Evening Star. The Stanways were a popular couple in Christchurch society. They were artistic, albeit English, and they were excused on this account for their noisy altercations. Moreover, Harriette was an inspired, if part-time, doctor: she could excise a tick and detect a louse better than anyone, and treat scabies and ringworm with something other than gentian violet, thus saving the children from much humiliation. She approached such problems with a horror and distaste equal to the children's own. She was rich, elegant and beautiful as well; fine-boned, clear-skinned and wide-eyed; unlike any doctor the New Zealanders – only later did they come to call themselves, self-dismissively, Kiwis – had met before, male or female, and she and Reg presented masques and gala operettas on the smooth banks of the river Avon, in the grounds of Bishop's House, which they rented from the Presbyterian Assembly. Reg, an altogether livelier and fleshier type than his wife, had sympathies with the unemployed and the underdog: he was known to have socialist tendencies. There was a rumour that he was Jewish and the name was originally Steinway, but no one had the heart to pursue it, to add this complication to those already in existence. By and large the couple presented so erratic a spectrum of attitude and behaviour, combined with so high a profile, the town just gave up bitching and forgave them their faults. Harriette's money and instinct for entertaining no doubt helped. The Stanways held parties in the grounds of Bishop's House; they employed domestic staff to keep the supply of vol-au-vents, eclairs and cheese straws flowing. Wine was all but unknown to the nation, not yet a hundred years old, but there was always beer, gin and whisky on offer and, what is more, and after the bars had closed as well. Closing time in those days was half past five in the afternoon, and a source of misery for everybody.

'You might well ask why, Cordelia, if Harriette hated the place and only Reg loved it, and Harriette had the money, did they stay in New Zealand? Why did Harriette not make a run for civilisation, get back to her academic and arty friends, her well-born, highly cultured family? Because in those days, Cordelia, women did not leave husbands; a divorce was a thing apart and a divorcee was a scarlet woman, and even Harriette was afraid. Besides, she loved him. And in those days men and women would fight and spat and there was no one to explain to them that such behaviour was unhealthy, or likely to upset the children.

'Was little Pippy much upset? Of course she was: children like to grow up into a happy world, Cordelia, and seldom do, though I can see you are doing your best for little Helen here. I think she's giving up: I think her eyes are closing. Today's children are reluctant to sleep, in case the world is different when they wake. Everything moves so fast. Then, it sauntered along.

'In the morning Pippy would watch her remorseful parents, Harriette's perfect face blotchily sullen, Reg's fleshy face so pale and stunned that the black hairs which sprouted round chin and jowls seemed more pronounced than ever. She'd watch them embrace, press into one another as if hoping to be the other, to get inside the other's skin, and it may have been that this upset her even more – both the inconsistency of their behaviour and the thought that love and hate are so closely linked. Pippy, like all children, longed for consistency, longed for justice, hoped to see virtue rewarded and wrong punished, and noted that only in story books was it ever so.

'By day, Harriette claimed it was love for Reg which kept her in New Zealand; by night she denied the love and gave as her reason that war in Europe was clearly on its way. The Germans would soon be at it again. How could she take Pippy into such a situation? – and where Harriette went Pippy went, no matter what Reg or the law had to say about the matter.

'By the time Pippy had got to be seventeen, the European war had indeed started, and there was then no way Harriette could get home even if she'd wanted to: ships no longer carried civilians, only troops from one war theatre to another. You could get by flying boat from Auckland to Sydney, but any further north than that and you would be mixed up in jungle warfare. The world was a much realer place in those days, Cordelia, and more dangerous, let me tell you. Distances meant something.

'How did Pippy get her name? She was called after the little shellfish which live on those Antipodean beaches, burying themselves in the fine dark damp sand just below the tide line – when the sea recedes you can tell their presence because they blow bubbles to the surface. Pipi-hunters watch and wait, and dig quickly where the tiny bubbles appear, and there they find them, solitary creatures, two little fine white fluted shells clamped together, and a delicate living morsel inside. Surely nothing dangerous can happen to it now it's safely closed? But it can, it can; it does. The pipi has betrayed itself, by breathing out.

'Pippy nearly got caught, couldn't help herself; betrayed herself by a breath of dangerous emotion. She was saved in the nick of time, oddly enough, by the most tremendous of Reg and Harriette's rows. Pippy, who later came to England and changed her name to Hypatia, and became a Greek scholar and married a clergyman, your grandfather, very nearly ruined her life. In those days it was easy for a girl to ruin her life. Now if a girl gets pregnant she can get unpregnant: if she gets married she can get unmarried. Money can save her from most disasters. But it was different then. Fall in love with the wrong man, and you'd had it for life.

'Pippy died before your mother Trixie gave birth to you, Cordelia. Do you have this family history straight? This child in its cradle, who in the modern fashion just won't go to sleep, is Pippy's great-grandchild. Harriette's great-great-grandchild. I'm no relative: I'm just a friend of the family. I carry its history in my head. Why are you confused? Didn't you know about the great Antipodean scandal? So great that poor Harriette and Reg were driven out of Bishop's House? On the positive side, it served to stop Pippy ruining her life. What opposed her, also saved her.

'I would have thought the present would relish this tale of the past: but on second thoughts no: the present relies on the past to exist as some boring and respectable country – a kind of New Zealand amongst other nations – by comparison to which they can see themselves as brave, daring and unconventional. Let me remind you, Cordelia, that the blood of Virginia Woolf runs in your veins, of cross-gendered folk with artistic abilities and infinite cultural grandeur, at least in their own eyes. Don't ever think you have your life in order: you won't have; there is too much trauma in your past, too much trouble in your genes for you to live the quiet life you occasionally think you want.

'When Pippy got to seventeen, she was in her last year of Christchurch Girls' High School, where scholastic standards were high. If Harriette had had her way, her daughter would have gone to St Margaret's, the town's fee-paying school, and worn a green uniform, or even Rangi-Ruru, up-country, and worn orange, but Reg insisted that the state grammar school and its navy blue was more ideologically sound. Not that the phrase was current then. "More appropriate to socialist principles" was how it was put.'

'Hypocrite!' Harriette would charge.

'Snob,' he'd respond.

'You don't mind living off my private income' – though 47

that would be hours into the quarrel – 'you just don't want Pippy to benefit from it! Pimp, gigolo!'

'Bitch.'

And so on. Reg won, and it ended up with Pippy at the Girls' High, wearing a navy blue gym tunic and a white shirt, chanting:

> 'Rangi-Ruri rotten rats,
> Do they stink? Yes, they do.
> Like the monkeys in the zoo!'

and falling hopelessly and unhealthily in love with a prefect, and writing her love letters which Harriette discovered, rifling through her drawers, as mothers did in those days without compunction.

'She's turning into a lesbian, Reg, but what did you expect? That school is a hell-hole of perversity!'

'Your side of the family, Harriette, not mine – a long line of lesbians –'

'Bastard! You'd rather score a point off me than look after your own child.'

'Harriette, can we calm down? She doesn't even know what men and women do together, let alone women and women.'

Which was true enough.

'It may have been Pippy's desire to prove to her mother that she was not a lesbian – in those days a source of shame, not pride – which led her to fall in love with Malcolm Mackay, a twenty-three-year-old farmer's son from Southland. His homestead was 100,000 acres of the plains south of Canterbury, a desolate land indeed: next stop Antarctica and the South Pole! Malcolm's father had died when his horse had stumbled and thrown him, its foot in a pothole, his head on a yellow-lichened stone. Now Malcolm helped his mother run the ranch, with its 100,000 sheep. One per acre. He had come by boat up the coast to Christchurch, quite openly looking for a wife to help his mother out, and his eye had, perversely enough, fallen upon Pippy. Perversely, I say, since in his head he wanted a good, stolid, no-nonsense, hard-working girl who could bake a dinner for a dozen sheep-shearers with one hand while making clothes for her kids with the other. But no, Cordelia, his eyes must fall upon your great-grandmother Pippy, who was petite, pretty, immensely clever, highly academic and carried an erotic charge she would not lose to the end of her days, and all sense deserted him. Her eye, alas, also fell upon Malcolm. He was well set up, and with a good mouth and chin, which many New Zealanders do not have. His teeth were firm, white and strong and all there – there is apparently a lack of iodine in that soil which makes good teeth a rarity. Many of Pippy's friends were given sets of false teeth by their fathers for their seventeenth birthday, and were overjoyed; the trouble and pain of a lifetime's dentistry spared them. Pippy and Malcolm clasped one another: his horny but young hands held her fine ones and – he in stumbling tones and she in poetic ones – they swore eternal love.'

'If you don't let me marry him,' said Pippy to Harriette, 'I'll   49 get pregnant by him. Then we'll all be up shit creek without a paddle!'

She'd talk like this to annoy Harriette and make Reg laugh. Getting pregnant was the threat girls held over their parents' heads in the days of respectability before contraception; when virginity was the good girl's path to future happiness.

'It's obviously true love,' said Reg to Harriette bitterly, 'and there's no escape from it. Bet you're sorry now your daughter doesn't take more after her Great-Aunt Virginia. Girls should marry young or they get ideas in their heads. But he's a nice steady young man, and it will do Pippy good to learn what real life is like.'

Though, actually, Reg too was appalled. But he didn't want Harriette to know. Or she'd have said (she did): 'This is what comes of sending her to a State school.'

The date of the wedding was fixed. It was to be a big do. The Southland relatives were to come up the coast, by the dozen; the cream of Christchurch society was to attend. The bride was to wear white, as befitted her virginal state: for the women, formal dress; for the men, white tie. Presents to Bishop's House, flowers by courtesy of the Christchurch Botanical Gardens: excitement was general, as Reg and Harriette, everyone agreed, were to be assimilated properly and finally into the community by way of Pippy.

Pippy stoutly maintained her love for Malcolm over the six months of the engagement, and he for her, though his mother, Mrs Matilda Mackay – her grandmother had come over from Scotland in one of the early waves of immigration – was shaken by her son's choice of bride. She doubted

Pippy could bake a decent sponge, let alone rear a lamb, or mend a tractor, or milk a cow, or any of the things Mrs Mackay did as of rote in her daily life. But perhaps the girl would learn. She'd have to. She'd be eighty miles from the nearest neighbour and there'd be no one to help, and no one to put on airs for, let alone Malcolm, who'd get tired of her nonsense after a week; that is, if he took after his father.

'You're so fragile, so perfect,' muttered Malcolm in Pippy's ear, and if he had a doubt or so, he subdued them.

'You're so strong and peaceful,' murmured Pippy in Malcolm's ear. 'I know we'll never quarrel. I'm sorry about my family. I know they're peculiar.'

'I can put up with them,' said Malcolm. 'They're pommies, and can't help it. But you're a regular bloke; you were born here, after all.'

'The day of the wedding dawned, as it should, bright and fair, and even the southern-west Arch had left the sky, which meant even the wind was on the young couple's side: zephyr-fresh, not at all hot and dusty. On days like this nature seemed to have forgiven the two islands (three if you include Stewart Island, that afterthought of an after-thought) for existing out of turn: indeed, even to want to make it up to the inhabitants. Up in the North Island, Mount Cook – in those days still perfectly formed; its main peak properly balanced by two smaller peaks: one was to blow itself up in the eighties, in the same way a foolish and careless terrorist can maim himself with his own explosives – Mount Cook, as I say, Cordelia, let off the merest wispy cloud of smoke to show it wasn't angry, merely alive – and the kiwis snuffled and grunted and came out from under cover, and one was captured by the Wellington Zoo, and the Taniwha – the Maoris' mythical monster – refrained from shaking the ground with his foot. That is to say there wasn't even an earthquake anywhere that day. Puff pastry rose properly in ovens, cream did not turn sour for no reason, sheep refrained from spraining their ankles in rabbit holes.

'But Harriette and Reg rowed on. Their anger with one another had not for once got appeased by sex, so great was their pre-nuptial anxiety. Wedding nerves! Forget Pippy, what about the parents?

'On the morning of the wedding, their clothes were laid out by the maid on the double bed in the spare room. (The maid, Ellie, was later to become an Olympic swimmer: she regularly kept wanting days off for practice, which Harriette would regularly refuse her: she did not follow the Stanways into exile, as they had expected her to do.) Reg's dress shirt was clean and starched: his tuxedo, with its purple cummerbund, all present and correct. Reg had had no occasion to wear it for some three years. The war had, to his relief, led to less formality in Canterbury society: it had taken a big wedding to restore it. A long time since an invitation had asked for formal attire.

'Harriette was to wear a little pale green silk suit, with gold-buttoned jacket and swinging skirt, and a dark green cloche hat with a veil. She had put on some weight lately; she had in fact to have the suit let out for the occasion. You don't understand "letting out", Cordelia? In those days clothes had hems and the seams were generous: they could be made bigger and smaller at will. You could get as much as four inches more round hips and waistband. Women *sewed*, Cordelia.'

The night had led to actual fisticuffs between the Stanway parents. Reg suddenly changed his position regarding the wedding and said he disapproved of the match; it made him sick to his heart. Pippy was ruining her life. He blamed Harriette; she had impetuously and unkindly accused Pippy of being a covert lesbian: now of course the girl was determined to leave home.

'You said she didn't know what I was referring to,' pointed out Harriette acidly, 'so how can I have upset her? If it's anyone's fault it's yours. You are much too possessive of her – it's unhealthy. Of course she has to leave home!'

And so it had begun. Harriette had become hysterical. She had slapped Reg: Reg had slapped her back. There had been much running around Bishop's House and slamming of doors all night while Pippy and the servants lay awake and listened, and longed for their beauty sleep.

Pippy herself had almost decided to call the marriage off; perhaps she need simply not show up at the ceremony? She was worried about her dress. Mrs Mackay had produced her grandmother's white – well, yellowy – wedding dress, circa 1860, and insisted that she wear it. It would save unnecessary expense, as well as being in the family tradition, though it turned out that Pippy was in fact the first Mackay bride small enough to get into the dress, for all its seams, since the original, wraith-thin, New Zealand Mackay had managed it. The dress seemed to Pippy to be   53 ill-omened, since the poor girl had died of TB within three years of her wedding: Malcolm and his mother both pooh-poohed her sensibilities. Pippy could see that her sensibilities would always be much pooh-poohed down on the farm. Perhaps her mother was right: perhaps she should not give up her education, her place at university? At Canterbury College, where the great Karl Popper lectured? Malcolm at least loved her; he did not see through her. If Pippy lost him, who would ever take her seriously again? The sound of the shrieks and the slamming doors on her pre-nuptial night made Pippy put away doubt. She would marry Malcolm Mackay first, worry second.

Eight o'clock in the morning came. The wedding was at eleven. The maids were up and about: the marquee was going up on the lawn: flower arrangements were in hand: caterers' vans delivered tables, chairs, even food; the Post Office delivered telegrams and presents. The hairdresser – only one in all the town, so sensible and practical were its inhabitants – had arrived to do the bride's and the bride's mother's hair. And still Reg and Harriette had not turned up to make their apologies and perform what Malcolm called their lovey-dovey act.

Pippy began to be worried. She felt tearful. Her hair was done: her mother's wasn't. She was in her dress. She even liked it. The vicar, Mr Hollycroft, turned up for a few last-minute instructions. He assured Pippy that the ceremony could take place without her parents if it came to it, since they had already signed the necessary consent forms. Nevertheless, he looked troubled. Were the Stanway parents ill? What was the matter? Shrieks and shouts could be heard from upstairs.

Mr Hollycroft and Pippy waited until the last moment, and then went upstairs to stand outside the spare-room door. Pippy knocked but was not heard. They listened.

'Bastard! You said I was fat!'

'I did not say you were fat. I said you were always too thin for my taste. That is wholly different.'

'I wish I'd never married you!'

'I assure you it is mutual.'

'You've ruined my life. You look ridiculous in a purple cummerbund. Dressed up like a monkey for these provincials.'

'At least I'm not bursting out of my clothes, as you are, Harriette. Look at you! It's absurd. The buttons will hardly meet. Put on something else decent, for God's sake.'

'I have nothing else decent. I suppose you want me to go naked.'

'I certainly don't want you to go naked. You don't have the figure for it.'

'You didn't care about my figure the night before last.'

'I kept my eyes shut. But then I always do these days. In bed with you, who would want to open them?'

And so on, and so on. And then, from Reg:

'Very well, I shan't wear a purple cummerbund. You are quite right, it makes me look ridiculous. I'm the one who's going naked to the wedding. Put that in your pipe and smoke it.'

And then, from Harriette:

'Then I'm not going at all. I am not going to stand and watch my daughter ruin her life at your behest.'

'At your behest, my dear, neither am I!'

The Reverend Hollycroft and Pippy crept away. Pippy struck away a tear or two, and Mr Hollycroft got hold of his brother to give the bride away.

'We'll say they've got food poisoning,' he said. 'People will understand. The important thing, my dear, is that for you this is a day to remember.'

Word was got to Malcolm, staying in the Cathedral Square Hostelry – Christchurch's one hotel – that the bride's parents had food-poisoning and were not going to the wedding.

'It's bad blood,' wept Mrs Mackay. 'You're marrying into bad blood. This wedding will be a disaster. You'll have peculiar children.'

'Peculiar', then as now, was about the worst thing you could say about anyone in New Zealand society. Malcolm was shaken but determined to go ahead.

'Look, Mum,' he said, 'it's her I'm marrying, not her parents.'

Pippy was standing at the altar when Malcolm walked up the aisle with his best man. He thought she looked perfectly lovely: his great-grandmother's wedding dress was just fine. Even he had had his doubts. Pippy glanced over her shoulder and dimpled at her husband-to-be. It was going to be all right. The church was packed with a congregation who also all surely knew, or they wouldn't have been there in their best bib-and-tucker, that it was going to be all right.

The groom stood by the bride's side. The Reverend Hollycroft began to speak. Then his voice faltered and stopped. The congregation rustled and murmured. Malcolm and Pippy turned.

Harriette and Reg stood in the entrance of the church: the door was open and bright antipoedean light shone upon them, dispelling all sepulchral gloom. The light in New Zealand is always bright: there's so much ocean all around for it to glance off. Reg slapped Harriette with his silver handbag. Harriette beat Reg about the head. Harriette was wearing Reg's tuxedo, cummerbund, white dress shirt, bow tie and all. She looked terrific. She had rolled up sleeves and trousers. She wore Reg's black polished shoes. And Reg, Reg was wearing Harriette's pale green suit: the gold-buttoned jacket was strained across his hairy chest; the pleated skirt came to just above the knee. His bare legs were sturdy and hairy. He wore her high-heeled pumps in apple-green satin. He wore her little cloche and veil, or had, except that now Harriette's blows had knocked it off. He held her hand aloft to stop her.

'Bastard!' said he to her.

'Bitch!' said she to him.

They realised where they were: a kind of sanity returned. They looked at one another, at the congregation, and decided they must go through with what they had begun. The quarrel was over: now they would have to act together. They walked up the aisle towards the altar. Mrs Mackay, in the front row, screamed her son's name aloud.

Pippy looked at Malcolm, Malcolm looked at Pippy. Malcolm dashed the ring he held in his hand to the ground, and turned and ran. Mrs Mackay ran after him: waddle, waddle, big strong hip this way, big strong hip that way, on unaccustomed high heels. Malcolm thrust Harriette and Reg apart as he ran: Mrs Mackay did the same. Reg and Harriette joined up again and went on walking altarward. The congregation's paralysis held until Reg and Harriette stood either side of Pippy. Then there was an unpleasant laughter, a tittering; cries of 'perverts', hisses, boos. The Reverend Hollycroft leaned back against his frugal altar, too appalled to quieten or calm his flock. His congregation departed, standing not upon the order of their going.

'Well,' said Harriette. 'That settled that.'

'It certainly did,' said Reg.

Both seemed rather amused. Pippy did what she should have done a long time back: she slapped them both, hard. First mother's cheek, then father's.

'There now, Cordelia, I think that child has gone to sleep at last. Why does my mind turn so resolutely to slapping? What happened next? The Reverend Hollycroft organised the distribution of the wedding bakemeats to the poor, the Mackays and their party retreated back to Southland, congratulating themselves on their lucky escape, and the Presbyterian Assembly did not renew its lease of Bishop's House. Harriette's patients no longer came for treatment; Reg was obliged to resign from his newspaper. The Stanways went to live in Wellington, that hilly, windy, rocking city, in modest retirement. The Taniwha seems to have a special down on Wellington.

'Yes, there was a great scandal. Pippy went on with her studies in Christchurch – the young are always more forgiving than the old: they have not yet discovered the necessity of condemnation – and took the first boat to England after the war, in 1946, to do her classical studies there. She became one of the first – and last – woman professors of Greek Literature in the world: the species was endangered, shortly to be extinct, but no one had told her that. All things change.

'Today Harriette and Reg could dress up in one another's clothes with impunity, and would not have to quarrel so much or so long to achieve their ambition. Pippy was later to say that that day of her almost-wedding, that parental quarrel which endured out of the night into the morning, that apotheosis of all previous rows, was what they had been moving towards all their married lives and had finally achieved. They were cross-dressers in a world in which the concept had not yet been verbalised.

'And, what is more, by facing their own natures, they saved Pippy from ruining her life. They changed the course of it. And just think, Cordelia, by so doing they allowed Trixie to come into existence, and after that you, and now this sweet little baby too. Though I always think a baby who cries and won't sleep when there is absolutely nothing wrong with it is simply egocentric.'

A Note on Fay Weldon

Fay Weldon was born in Birmingham, brought up in New Zealand, and educated at Hampstead School for Girls. At the age of twenty, armed with an MA from St Andrews in Economics and Psychology, she went to the Job Centre and was given work at the Foreign Office shuffling papers that sent spies to an uncertain fate in the East Bloc. She left when pregnant with the first of her four sons, and subsequently worked for a succession of leading advertising agencies in increasingly exalted positions. Since then she has become one of Britain's leading literary writers, screenwritten successfully for film and television, and in her journalism acquired a reputation for wit and controversy. Her work sells worldwide in translation. After a highly acclaimed BBC television adaptation, *The Life and Loves of a She-Devil* was made into a Hollywood film starring Roseanne Barr and Meryl Streep. She is a prolific writer, in the tradition of Dickens, concerned with social questions, but also believing that readers should have a good time when turning the page. She comes from a family of writers, but endured a decade of odd jobs and hard times as what today is called an unsupported mother, before starting to write. She is technically Dr Fay Weldon, MA, D Litt, with two honorary degrees from both the University of Bath and her alma mater, St Andrews. Her latest novel is *Splitting*.